FARMER BROWN

TOAD
HALL

TNI HII

LE'S
USE

Book Club Edition

WALT DISNEY PRODUCTIONS
presents

The
New Adventures
of Mr. Toad

Random House 🏠 New York

Copyright © 1983 by Walt Disney Productions. All rights reserved under International and Pan-American Copyright Conventions. Published in the United States by Random House, Inc., New York, and simultaneously in Canada by Random House of Canada Limited, Toronto. ISBN: 0-394-86320-8

Manufactured in the United States of America
34567890   ABCDEFGHIJK

One summer morning Mole
went to see his good friend Rat.
"It's a beautiful day for
a picnic, Ratty," said Mole.
"So it is," said Rat. "Let's
take my boat out on the river."

Before long Rat was ready.
He handed a picnic basket to Mole.
Then they rowed down the river.

The two friends ate their lunch
in the shade of a willow tree.

"Ah, this is the life!" said Rat.

"Yes," said Mole. "Lots of food
and no fuss and bother."

On the way home they passed Toad Hall.
Their good friend Mr. Toad lived there.
"I wonder how Toad is," said Rat.
"He has been awfully quiet."
"He must be keeping his promise," said
Mole. "He is staying out of trouble."

But Toad was not keeping his promise!
He had just bought a new motor car.
And for Toad, a car was trouble!

Toad loved
to drive.
But he was
a terrible driver.
He went too fast.
He stopped for nothing.
He was a terror on the road!

Toad pulled up in front of Toad Hall.
He leaped from his car.
"I must get hold of Mole and Ratty,"
he said. "They will love my new car!"

Toad rushed into the house.
He threw off his driving clothes.

Then he sat down at his desk
and wrote a letter to his friends.

Late that day Rat and Mole.
got back to Rat's house.
  They found a letter tucked
in the door.

Rat opened
the letter.
It said:

Dear Friends,
    Please come to tea
tomorrow.
    I have a surprise for
you.
            Toad

All evening Mole and Rat worried about
Toad's surprise.

"What can Toad be up to now?" said Mole.
"We had better talk to MacBadger," said
Rat. "He knows how to handle Toad."

The next day Mole and Rat went to visit MacBadger.

They showed him Toad's letter.

"I'm sure Toad is up to no good," said MacBadger. "I'll go with you."

Toad met his friends outside Toad Hall.
"Hello, hello!" cried Toad. "Look at
my new motor car! Isn't it grand?"

"What are you thinking of, Toad!"
said MacBadger. "You know you are
a terrible driver. Remember what
happened last time. You wrecked
your car!"

"This time will be
different," said Toad.
"I promise to drive
carefully. Come on,
I'll show you. Let me
take you for a ride."

Only Rat and Mole would get in the car.
Toad drove off.

"Nothing good
will come of this,"
said MacBadger.

And nothing good
did come of it.

Toad drove faster and faster.
"Slow down, Toad!" said Rat.
But Toad did not listen.

"Isn't this fun!"
cried Toad.
"Look out!"
yelled Rat.

The car ran off the road.
It crashed into Farmer Brown's fence.
The three friends flew out of the car...

. . . and landed on
a haystack.

The car was wrecked
but no one was hurt.
"I've had enough!"
said Rat.
And he and Mole
marched away.

Farmer Brown was very angry with Toad.
"You've ruined my fence!" he yelled.
But Toad was not listening.

Toad had spotted
the farmer's new
motorcycle.

"Here! I'll pay!"
Toad said.
And he did.

Toad paid for the fence.
And he bought the farmer's
motorcycle!

Toad hopped on
the motorcycle and
roared off.

The motorcycle was even
more fun than a car.
Toad zoomed along the roads.
He frightened all the animals.

ROAD OUT

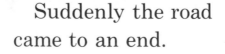

Suddenly the road
came to an end.

The motorcycle stopped.
But Toad did not.

That evening Mole and Rat sat peacefully
by the fire.

"Toad should be all right for a while,"
said Mole. "He doesn't have a car anymore."

Just then there
was a knock.

MacBadger came
running in with
the newspaper.

"Have you heard
what happened to
Toad?" he said.

The newspaper gave the bad news.
Toad was in the hospital.

"Oh, dear. Poor Toad," said Mole.
"We'll have to go and see him."

The next day the friends visited
Toad in the hospital.
Toad had broken his foot.

"It's really not so bad," said Toad.
"Just a little accident."

"You can't go on
like this, Toad!"
said MacBadger.
"You've got to
mend your ways!"

"You're right,"
said Toad. "I've
learned my lesson."

Soon Toad's friends left.
"A broken foot," said Mole. "Poor Toad
won't go anywhere for a while."

Toad was bored.
He hated staying
in bed.

That evening a nurse left a wheelchair
outside his room.
"Wheels!" said Toad.
He hopped out of bed and went to look.

On the wheelchair were
a lady's robe and nightcap.
They gave Toad an idea.

Toad put on the clothes.
"No one will know me!"
he said.

Then Toad climbed into the wheelchair.
He pushed on the wheels.
The wheelchair moved!

EXIT

The wheelchair was great fun.
And now Toad could get out of
the hospital!
All he had to do was follow
the red arrows.

EXIT ➡

A kind guard opened a door for Toad.
"Good evening, ma'am," the guard said.
Toad kept following the red arrows.
He found the back door of the hospital
and escaped!

Toad wheeled himself through
the moonlit countryside...
all the way back to Toad Hall.

Over at Rat's house, Toad's friends
were drinking cocoa and talking.

"Thank goodness Toad wasn't hurt badly,"
said Mole.

"Thank goodness he's stuck in bed for
a while," said Rat.

"Thank goodness he can't drive with
a broken foot!" said MacBadger.

The next day the friends
went fishing on the river.

Everything was peaceful
and quiet.

But then a noise broke
the stillness.

A motorboat was speeding up
the river.

The noise got louder and louder.

With a roar, the motorboat passed
close by.

It upset the rowboat!

Who was the careless driver?

It was Toad!

"Ahoy there!" he called. "How do you like my new boat? Isn't it grand?"

Toad waved happily to his friends.

He would never change!

MacBADGER'S HOUS

RATTY'S HOUSE